My Father
the Great Pirate

In memory of Piero. MQ

First published in English in 2014 by Wilkins Farago Pty Ltd (ABN 14 081 592 770)
PO Box 78, Albert Park, Victoria, 3206, Australia
Teachers' Notes & other material: www.wilkinsfarago.com.au

© 2013 orecchio acerbo s.r.l.
viale Aurelio Saffi, 54 - 00152 Roma

© 2013 Davide Cali (for text)
© 2013 Maurizio A.C. Quarello (for illustrations)
© 2014 Wilkins Farago (English translation)

Wilkins Farago would like to thank Julian Maiolo for his assistance with the English translation.

A CIP record for this title is available from the National Library of Australia

Printed in China by Everbest Printing Co Ltd

ISBN 978-0-9871099-9-6

MY FATHER

THE GREAT

PIRATE

A TALE BY DAVIDE CALI · IILUSTRATED BY MAURIZIO A.C. QUARELLO

wf

WILKINS *farago*

When I was a child, my father went away.
He came home only once a year, for two weeks in the summer.
He smelled of the sea, my father. That's because he was a pirate.

A great pirate.

After he arrived home, my father would take me on his knee,
open up a big map that smelled of dust,
and would show me all the places where he had been.
For each place, he would tell me of a ship he'd attacked,
and how many times they'd decided to spare some sailors' lives
in exchange for all the treasure they had.

However, he never brought any treasure home.
"Papa, why don't you bring home any treasure?" I asked him.
He began to laugh:
"Because the treasure's in a safe place
that only myself and The Tattooed One know about. That's why!"

and I knew everyone's name.

The Tattooed One was a pirate covered in tattoos who never said a word.
Dollar, the parrot, spoke for him instead.
Then there was **Tobacco**, who cooked well and told some spine-tingling ghost stories;
and **The Beard** who, they say, had been hairy since he was a boy; and
Shorty, who wasn't afraid of anything, even though he was only as tall as a child.

And then there was **Figaro** (they called him that because he was once a barber), who played the accordion and cried like a baby every full moon.

And **The Turk**, who was as strong as a tree trunk and had once fought a swordfish with his bare hands (and it still bore the scars). He was also so delicate he was left to mend the sails when they were torn by the wind.

Sou'wester was famous for passing wind at night.

Then there was **Sausage**, who smelled like a damp cellar and on stormy nights would bring out sausages made by his sister back in his home town, which were all fatty and spicy.

My father always brought home a gift

for me.

When I was seven,

he brought back

a pirate flag

The Turk had sewn

especially for me.

Every year, when he returned, I asked my father to recount tales about

... about how **The Tattooed One** had found a girlfriend but she wanted him to remove his tattoos ...

... of **Tobacco**, who thought he'd seen a ghost on the bridge but later discovered it was only a piece of cloth ...

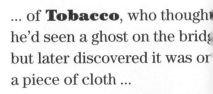

is pirate crew. I'd fall asleep listening to the sound of his voice and stories ...

of **The Beard**, who had his [be]ard shaved off by the crew one [ni]ght only for it to grow back by [th]e next morning ...

... of **Shorty**, who had once met the Devil and asked to borrow money from him ...

... and of **Figaro**, who had cut the hair of the king's son so badly he was forced to run away.

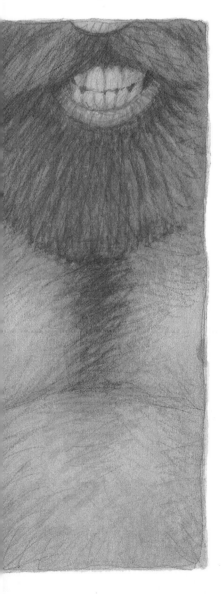

And then of the **The Turk**, who had once eaten a lobster still in its shell for a bet ...
of **Sou'wester**, who asked a sorceress to cure his flatulence
and she replied that it would take a miracle ...
Sausage, who found a cat had eaten his sausages, so he ate the cat ...
And **Dollar**, named by The Tattooed One because he would always say:
"If I had a dollar for every time he squawked, I'd be rich!"

And about his ship, called *Hope*.

"Why *Hope*?" I asked. He answered me:

"We hope to return home."

When I was nine years old, my father didn't return home for the summer.

A telegram arrived one morning.

After reading it, my mother simply said,
"We have to make a trip."
"Where are we going?"
"To Papa."

I imagined a journey by ship, but no.

Mum hardly said a thing during the journey.
Every now and then, I looked for the sea out of the window but never saw it.
On the second night, I asked my mum if Dad was still far away.
She said we would see him the following morning and I fell asleep, convinced
I would be awakened by the sea.

I realised something had happened to my father even
though Mum had not told me anything.

But what? This, I couldn't know.
Perhaps his ship had sunk?

That night, I had a dream.

When I opened my eyes, it was still dark outside. We had stopped.
Inspectors entered the compartment to check our travel documents.
The journey lasted for many more hours.
When we finally got off the train, there was still no sea.

It was a place called Belgium.

Sometimes in your dreams, you see the future before it happens,
or you can see what happens to your loved ones.
By this time, I expected my father to be dead.
So, when the hospital asked if I wanted to see
my father, I said no: the dead scared me.
My mother pushed me into the room.
I closed my eyes and went inside.

My father was not dead.

He was all bandaged up. But you could tell it was him from the sound of his breathing.
Nobody said a thing. My mother left the room and I heard her talking to someone.
I stood in front of my father and called to him two or three times.
But, just like in a dream, he slept on.
In the car, I heard mother say something about a collapse, but I didn't understand.
I didn't know where she was taking me, and so I asked.
My mum just said: "You'll see."

A lady led us to a room with two beds. My mother finally spoke to me:

"This is the place
where your father works.
Not precisely here, but not far away.

He is a miner.

They descend hundreds of metres
underground
and down there, they
dig
and bring out the coal.
Three days ago, the mine
collapsed.
Your father was lucky.
Others
didn't
make
it."

I remember that day well, because I found my father alive when I expected him to be dead.

And because it was the day I realised I was no longer a child.

The next morning, my father was awake.
I moved closer to him and suddenly he looked like a stranger I had never seen before.
The fact was he had told me a pack of lies.

He wasn't a pirate, there wasn't a ship called *Hope*, or hidden treasure, or fights with sharks.

My father, the pirate, had truly died.

I had found a different father.
A brave father who dug underground in the dark and without air,
but one who told lies.
And I didn't know if I could love him.

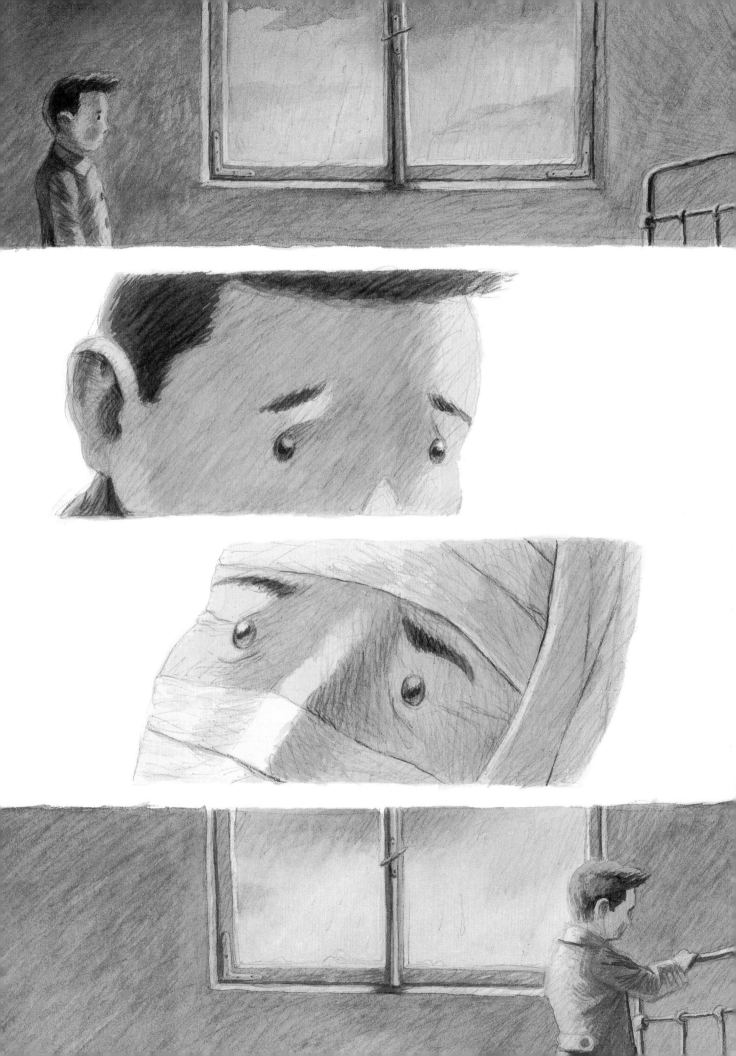

In the afternoon, we were taken to the mine.
A bearded man accompanied us to my father's hut.
It was dark inside but I recognised the picture on the wall.

Outside, my father's workmates were waiting for us.

Just as we were leaving, I caught a glimpse of a big green tattoo beneath the shirt of one of them.

Nothing more was spoken about the mine

We returned home, and after a month we were joined by my father.

After that summer, he never left us again and I loved him as much as I had before.
But for many years I couldn't understand the reason for those lies.

until the day a letter arrived.

That night, my father went down to the basement and stayed there a long time.
When it was time for dinner, I went to call him and found him looking inside an old suitcase.
There was his helmet and lamp from the time he worked in the mines.
"What is that?" I asked.
"A sextant. It helps sailors navigate the seas at night using the stars," said my father. "As a young man, I wanted to be a sailor, but there were no seaports near where I was born. There wasn't even work. When they told me I could have a job, but that it was far away, I couldn't believe it. I wanted to go away, to explore the world, but there weren't any ships or seas to explore in the place I ended up working. A Greek guy gave me the sextant: he had travelled a long way to work in the mines, too."

That evening, I finally began to understand.

My father hadn't lied to me at all. He really had wanted to work at sea. Perhaps he held that dream for years so he didn't have to think about having to go underground. Maybe he couldn't go back down each day without those dreams.

The letter was a notice that the mine was closing.
The miners had continued to work in the mine where my father was almost buried,
but now there was no more coal left.
The letter was sent by an old friend.
The miners were going to bid farewell to the mine for the last time.

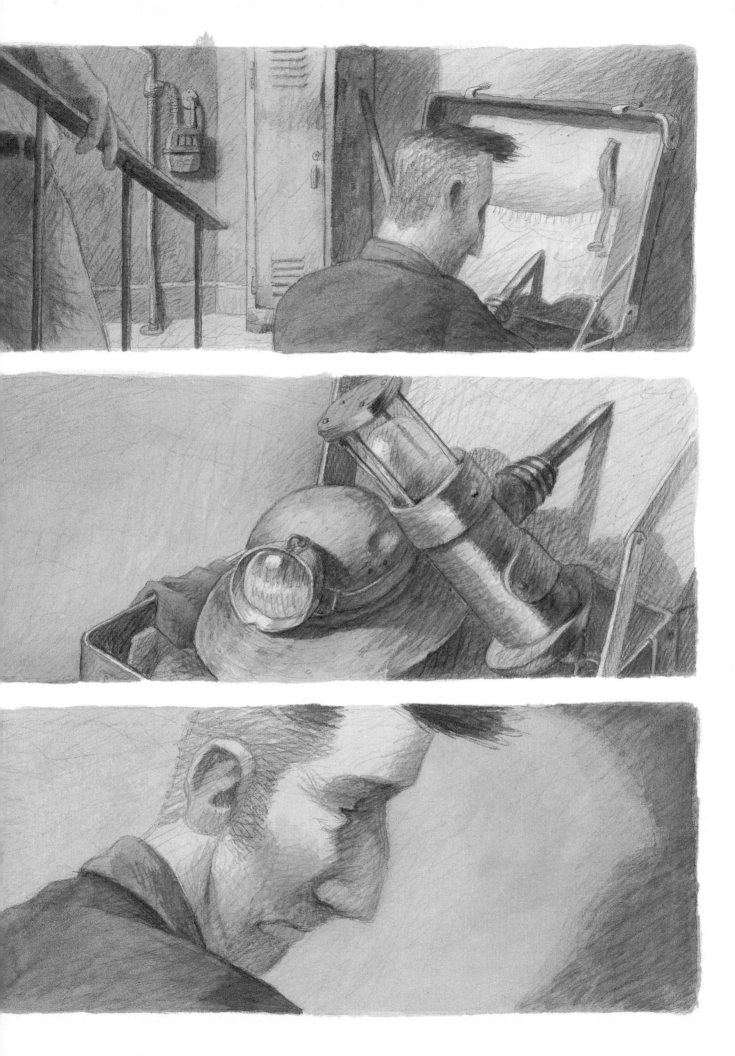

We returned to Belgium.

The trip didn't seem as long this time but, like the first time, no-one spoke a word for nearly the entire trip.
It seemed a happy occasion to me: my father was going to meet old friends he hadn't seen for years.

No one came to meet us at the station.
We stayed at a small hotel.
A very nice lady prepared onion soup for us for dinner.

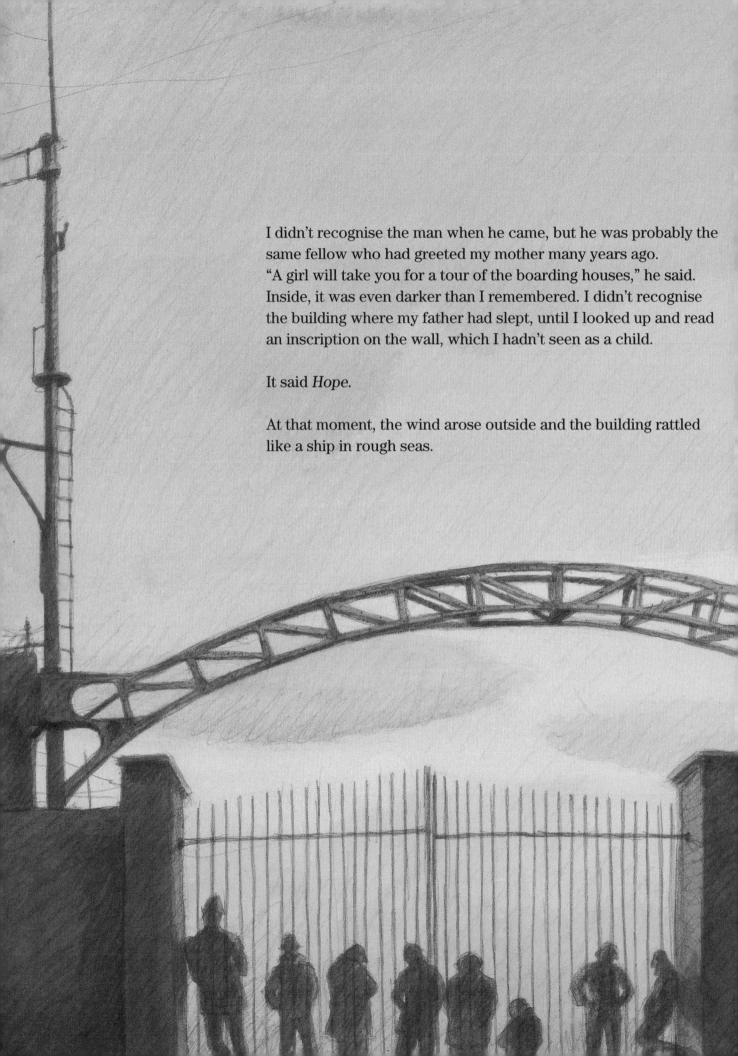

I didn't recognise the man when he came, but he was probably the same fellow who had greeted my mother many years ago.
"A girl will take you for a tour of the boarding houses," he said.
Inside, it was even darker than I remembered. I didn't recognise the building where my father had slept, until I looked up and read an inscription on the wall, which I hadn't seen as a child.

It said *Hope.*

At that moment, the wind arose outside and the building rattled like a ship in rough seas.

The tour continued in silence, almost like a

Outside the mine, they all began to cry.

The monster that
had swallowed
them up and spat them
out again for all those years
was finally closing, yet
they wept for those
who remained below,
and also for themselves.
For they had left their youth
down there too.

I watched them and I still did not understand,
until, beneath the half-open shirt of one of them,
I noticed the tattoo I had seen
so many years before.

isit to a cemetery.

I looked at them one by one and I marvelled

They were all there:
The Tattooed One, **Tobacco**, **The Beard**, **Shorty**,
Figaro, **The Turk**, **Sou'wester**, **Sausage**.

Only **Dollar** was missing.

that I hadn't recognised them before.

They were all there, the crew of dirty pirates crying like children in front of their ship.
The ship which had faced so many storms, in a sea that had taken so many of them away.
They had come to say goodbye forever.
They could not hate her, because she had given them hope when they had none.

At that point, I realised that there was something I had to do.

On the evening we had received the letter, I had found something in the cellar.
Before leaving home, I had put it in my suitcase.

I climbed to the top of the tower and, before I took it out,
I looked down for a moment.

I met my father's eyes and for the first time, after so many years,
I saw him as I remembered him.
My father, the great pirate.

He had never left.

HISTORICAL NOTE FOR PARENTS, TEACHERS AND OLDER READERS

This story is inspired by real events.

After the Second World War (1939–1945), there were few jobs in Italy (and many other European countries).

People needed to work to survive, however, and hundreds of thousands of Italians left their own country for Germany, Belgium, France, Switzerland (where Davide Cali was born), and even the United States of America and Australia.

In the 1940s and 1950s, Italy signed agreements with Belgium to send Italian workers to dig for coal in Belgium's coal mines. In exchange, Italy would be able to buy coal from Belgium at cheaper prices.

None of the workers knew they'd be working a thousand metres underground. Like thousands of others, they just left their home country hoping for a better life. By the mid-1950s, around 40% of all coal miners in Belgium were Italian.

In 1956, a fire in a coal mine in Marcinelle, Belgium, killed 262 miners, 136 of them Italian migrants. Only 13 workers survived. It is still remembered as one of Italy's worst mining disasters.

Today, a museum sits on the site of the old mine at Bois du Cazier. It is a UNESCO World Heritage site.

Several of Maurizio A. C. Quarello's illustrations for this book were inspired by photographs of the Marcinelle coal mine.

www.wilkinsfarago.com.au